# The Audition

## A Naughty Gay Short

by

**R. W. Clinger**

Paxtonian Publishing
955 Bayridge Avenue
Pittsburgh, PA 15226

The Audition – A Naughty Gay Short
Copyright 2021 – R. W. Clinger
First Edition

1234567890

Made in the USA

Cover art provided by K. Padilla Inc.
Models (int./ext.): Matt Desmond / Rick Daye

# The Audition

## A Naughty Gay Short

# Also by R. W. Clinger

---

# The Audition

## A Naughty Gay Short

*For Lance Zarimba*

# JULY 16

# RIDING

Hotter than the Mojave Desert outside. Breaking high temperatures. Melting Earth heat. It doesn't stop me from my current task. No way. Come on … Take a peep with me … Look and learn …

*Ride. Ride. Ride.*

This is what I see, gawk at, study inside Corbin Casp's bedroom. My current boyfriend is naked and sweaty. The black-haired and blue-eyed beauty is riding uncut dick again, bouncing up and down on the slab of thick meat, and looking as if he's having the fucking time of his life.

*Up. Down. Up. Down. Up. Down.*

Corbin's twenty-eight-year-old cock—hard as steel and porn-perfect—slaps his stomach as he flies north and south like a goddamn pogo stick. While he bounces up and down, he calls out to the blond underneath him, "Fuck me! Fuck me hard!" Corbin faces away from his fucker. His smooth pecs glisten in the afternoon sunbeams and his pink nipples are about as hard as diamonds. One of his muscled arms reaches behind him and holds on to his Fontaine Amish headboard—the same headboard I've held onto plenty of moments while banging his bottom numerous times in our two-year relationship. He arches his neck and back, having the time his life as the blond goes to town on his tight, whore-rear.

*Up. Down. Up. Down. Up. Down.*

*Ride. Ride. Ride.*

Corbin's obviously having the fucking time of his life. Wish I had the blond's dick inside me.

# THE BANGER

This is our new game as Corbin's boyfriend. He wants me to watch him have sex with the blond underneath him and become hard between my legs. He wants me to unload cream inside my shorts.

I give Corbin credit, but just a miniscule amount. The banger behind him, licking his back once … twice … three times, is a total fucking stud: jock-perfect with a Superman-size chest covered in white-blond hair, broad shoulders, twilight-blue eyes, cords on his neck, ripped stomach, thick thighs, totem pole-size dick, and hands about as big as footballs. He has Corbin clamped by the hips, *bang … bang … banging* my boyfriend's bottom again and again and again. The blond looks like a rugby player all the way. He *is* a rugby player because there's a gold-black-white rugby jersey on the floor, a pair of size twelve cleats, and a rugby ball next to Corbin's dresser. The blond is a beautiful banger from head to toes. A model of sorts with lots of meat on his bones. Porn material with mounds of flowing and almost-white, super pale muscles.

I watch his condom-covered and massive post slide inside Corbin's rear, pull out, punch inside my man again, and continue this act for the next six … seven … eight minutes …

Corbin winks at me. Blows me a kiss.

I feel pre-shoot in my shorts. My balls tingle. Our game continues.

# INTUITION

Where am I? On Deona Street in downtown Templeton, next to Lake Erie in Pennsylvania. Outside the Radsha Building on the fourth floor fire escape, looking inside apartment 43, Corbin's place for the last six years. Spying on Corbin Casp and his blond, new street-find. Watching the pair as our game continues, getting hard as the two men fuck each other, ready to churn out a sticky load against my thick thighs.

Corbin's been seeing this rugby beefster for maybe the last three weeks. And he shares him with me. Corbin rides my dick up his ass. And he rides the rugby player's dick. It's a share-and-share-alike kind of thing that seems to be working out just fine lately. It's all dick-to-bottom grinding stuff among the three of us for twenty-one days now—I've kept track! A threesome galore!

Something I don't have a problem with. Activities that I enjoy. Our trio. Our game. Corbin. The blond. Me.

# *FINN*

*Ride. Ride. Ride.*

They become similar to wild animals on the bed. Sweaty. Bouncing together. Huffing. Puffing. Grunting like naked beasts. Both their faces turn a fiery red. The queen-size bed sounds as if it is going to break beneath their up-and-down weight.

*Ride. Ride. Ride.*

Corbin grabs the veined and fully erect tool at his center, jostles it up and down, up and down, up and down, consistently, with his meaty, right palm. He exclaims, having puffed cheeks, and the widest eyes, "Going to blow, Finn!"

The banger is German. The blond is from a part of Germany called Bavaria. Finn is here in the US on a Green Card. No surprise since Corbin has always liked his German men, and blonds, and rugby players. No surprise at all. Hell, I'm German. Karl Meader at your service. This is me.

# KOMMEN

Finn blasts my boyfriend's rear with thrust after thrust after thrust. They are wicked bolts. Powerful ones that can take down the building. The German grinds his teeth behind Corbin's muscled back and has at my once-lover's ass.

Corbin huffs ... puffs ... huffs and shoots his creamy, white boys everywhere: on the sheets, against Finn's feet, over his chest, and in his own face. He always empties his load like this, makes a mess, ever since the first time we had sex. Never fails. Blows his shit everywhere. I mean *everywhere*!

"Kommen," Finn growls. I know very little German, but translate this as *coming*. Finn continues to pound ... pound

… pound Corbin's buttocks, closes his eyes, and barks, "Kommen! Kommen! Kommen!"

# SEX FIENDS

I don't stay and watch their post-sex play; I have shit to do. I'm sure they have shit to also carry out: it probably will consist of cigarettes and shots of warm Jagermeister to celebrate their love for each other. Usually I will climb through the window and join them in a hug on the bed, and some heavy kissing. Each will take turns blowing me until I get off. This time, I leave them be and head down the fire escape, into the rest of my summertime day, and need to return to my place, back to work.

Truth is, I'll get off with the men later. Both are sex fiends and will have at each other again, and my bare skin. I'll be in the mix of their gig and we'll process a sexy, heated, and sticky threesome later. Hell yeah we will. It's what we do. It's our gig. Us.

# MY PLACE

I head home. What's a guy to do after playing a watching fuck-game with his boyfriend and a handsome, German, blond rugby player, right? You don't have to answer this. I already know the answer.

My flat is simple. Small with four rooms. The basics. It does have a killer view of Lake Erie. I've thought about moving into a condominium, or buying a Tudor, cottage, or saltbox nearby, which I can afford and modestly live in, but honestly, I've fallen in love with the flat, city life next to the swelling and falling lake, and Templeton. Kudos to me. So, I'll be staying right here for a while at 782 Piffin Street, flat 6. Come and visit if you'd like. Who knows, you might just have a good time with me, and my two boyfriends?

# DIRTY

I don't feel dirty after watching Corbin and Finn have pounding sex. Should I? Truth is, I love to watch my man getting banged by the German dude we fuck together. It's a total turn-on for me. It's bliss. Some guys wouldn't be able to handle having a third man in a relationship, but Corbin and I are falling for Finn. He's perfect for us: caring, thoughtful, charming, honest, aggressive when he needs to be, sweet, and trusting. He's a good find for us. A strong match. The best lover. And the perfect addition to our fuck-marathons.

I don't get started on work right away. Instead, I climb into the shower, scrub down a few times, stand under the hot spray, and recall …

I didn't meet Corbin at bar or book signing, or while jogging, or online. Nothing like that happened. Lucy set us up. Lucy Ping. My bestie for the last two hundred years. She lives upstairs in flat 7. The sweetheart has a better view than me, but whatever.

Lucy works for Vanda Mars, the uppity interior decorator here in Templeton. Vanda is Corbin's cousin. You see how this is unfolding, of course. Corbin was single. Vanda was looking out for Corbin's dick. Vanda got Lucy to ask me to go out with Corbin. Maybe I could suck his dick or something. Blah. Blah. Blah. It all worked out.

# LUCY

My cell phone pulls me out of my memories and the shower. I turn off the knobs, stop the spray, and step out of the shower. I snag a towel, my phone on the sink, and see Lucy Ping's face on my screen: Asian-American, petite, thirty this year, a fresh newlywed to a wealthy and uppity banker named Lee Chow.

"Lucy, I'm naked," I say, answering her call. "But I'm not hard."

"Not with Corbin … or Finn?"

"Not with Corbin or Finn," I repeat, shaking my head.

"I'm at work. Let me make this quick. How'd did the fire escape mission go on Deona Street? Was it as *hot* as last time?"

"Yes. The German knows what he's doing in the bedroom department and ..."

"You're falling for him. Corbin and you both are," she cuts me off. I can always count on Lucy being blunt and to the point. No frills, all thrills. I must renew her bestie friendship card for the next two years, or longer.

"Yes. Maybe. I'm not sure. It's so fresh. Only twenty-one days. I really don't know what to expect emotionally yet. He's easy to fall for, though."

"I think it's perfectly fine to fall for Finn. He seems genuine and sweet. And he's honest. Threesomes work because of honesty. I don't object to such relationships. Love is love is love."

"How do you know this?"

She giggles. "Let's just say that I've had my share … Which I should probably tell Lee about before marrying him."

"How many threesomes have you had?"

"Two. In college. A few drinks. A few guys. A few girls. You know how it goes. I'm not a Japanese angel. Most people think I am, but they're wrong."

"I guess so. I've always loved your stories, Lucy. You never surprise me."

I hear Vanda Mars screaming something behind Lucy. Lucy immediately whispers into her phone, "Gotta run. Later, love. The demon queen rises."

"Chat soon," I reply, end the call, realizing that Lucy has to get back to work.

# PUZZLING

I decide to work a few hours at my tiny desk that overlooks Piffin Street and the lake. I have the greatest job on the planet. You can never guess what is. Never! I work for Pagoda Puzzles. It's owned by Mark and Luther Pagoda. The married couple is now in their late sixties, still located here in Templeton. The company has been around since 1982. Most puzzlers compare Pagoda to Springbok, and call the puzzles:

"Sturdy … The highest standard in puzzles on the market today."

"You get top quality, exactly what you pay for."

"A challenge in every box … Dependable fun for family and friends."

My job is simple: I get to thumb through dozens of colored photographs on my laptop and decide which are best for puzzle builders. Cats. Dogs. Pandas. Palm trees. Sunsets. Rainbows. Thumbtacks and rulers. Lizards. Cowboys. Leprechauns. Coffee shops. Balloons. Birthday parties. Candy bars. Pies. Flowers. Swans. Frogs. Children playing. Princes. Princesses. Castles. Spaceships. Aliens. Football players. Beach scenes. Volcanoes. Yarn stores. Book covers. Pillows. Blankets. Farmers. Corn fields. Sunflowers. Stereo systems. Pictures. Gates. Bridges. Cement sidewalks. And just about anything your imagination can derive.

Plus, I'm sometimes instructed to put two or three pictures together, like: umbrellas and rainstorms, baseballs and backyards, coins and lottery machines, parking tickets and policewomen. Yin and Yang pieces. You get the idea.

Rarely, am I'm called into the office at 63 Chowd Way, which is walking distance from my flat. Mostly our office meetings are held on Zoom.

Another one of my duties, which is required by ten percent of Pagoda employees, is to build one puzzle a week. Whether it's a Pagoda Puzzle, or one from a competitive company. Notes are mandatory regarding the building process. Notes must include: Are the pieces easy to handle? Do the pieces stay together? Is the box sturdy? Does the picture on the outside of the box help the puzzler? Is there puzzle dust in the bottom of the box? Does the puzzle come with a pamphlet/catalog of other puzzles to purchase? And other various questions that need to be completed while building.

I get busy. A 1000-piece puzzle sits on a card table next to my slim desk. Better get building and note taking.

*Work. Work. Work.*

# DRAGON NEAR PETE'S DINER

I probably slip together 200 pieces of the 1000-piece puzzle titled *Princess Castle on Lake Erie*. The puzzle is a copy of an oil painting that was originally created by the local artist Dean Sinclair. Pagoda has an entire series of the artist's oil pieces created into puzzles: *Unicorn by Lighthouse, Fire-Breathing Dragon Along Interstate, Knights of the Round Table Climb Jungle Gym, Merlin Over Lake, Dragon Near Pete's Diner*. The puzzles sell very well. Sinclair, of course, makes a portion of Pagoda's profits, most of which he donates to The Templeton Foundation of Arts, his charity.

Following my puzzling, I choose three kitten (all white, long-haired, fuzzy, and blue-eyed) photographs to send via email to my supervisor, Kim Shredder, at Pagoda. She will pick one of the three (or maybe all three) for the creation of a puzzle in the near future. Hereafter, I find myself at the floor-to-ceiling (a tiny flat, but with such a massive view, if you recall) window, peer down at Piffin Street and see all the small people walking about. Ants here and there. People/ants. My mind strays to a new set of puzzles for Pagoda which I might have to talk to Kim about. *Hmmmmm*.

# BLITZ

I've never handled my alcohol well. Never.
Not since I was sixteen and attended my first
beer parties at Fern Hill Park. Not now at
thirty-four. I get drunk quick and become
silly and sloppy and fun. I always know
what's going on around me, though. And I
don't slur my words. But everyone present
can tell that I'm inebriated; something I can
never hide.

Lucy visits me after work. "You're
fucked up. What have you been doing since
I called you earlier? Did you have a one-
man party?"

I tell her about work, work, and
work.

"You're boring as fuck, Karl." She looks at the semi-empty bottle of Absolut on the counter and my shot glass. She helps herself to a shot.

"Stay for a few more shots."

"I can't. Lee is taking me out for Italian. We might see a movie. Who knows," she winks at me, "we might just skip a movie."

"Sounds fun."

"What are you going to do? Drink more? Sleep off your blitz? Build more of your puzzle?"

I shrug. "Who knows? Something. I'll sober up a touch. There's the new Grisham I want to start. Or I'll cruise Netflix."

She helps herself to another shot of vodka, warming up her evening. Lucy can drink, unlike me. She can put the alcohol away, unaffected by the shit. Good for her. Sad for me. "I'm sure you'll keep yourself busy."

"I will."

"Will Corbin and Finn stop by?"

I shake my head. "I doubt it. They mentioned being alone this evening. Not that I mind. I get it. The three of us don't have to be together *all* the time."

She agrees. "Grisham is a fine man. You'll do well with him."

And our conversation ends, because she has to get ready for her date with Lee, her fiancé, and whatever she intends to do with the banker … all night long.

# UNEXPECTED VISIT

Okay. Okay. I'm not a drinker. Not usually. I drink socially and that's about it. I get carried away, though. Out of control. I drink even more after Lucy leaves. Just because. No reason. I have three more shots of vodka and … take a long, long, long nap. I fall into my queen-size platform bed and sort of pass out. When I come to, Corbin stands overtop me. He's naked and fully erect. Such a handsome man. Chiseled. Just right for my needs. All muscle and toned. Someone who cares about his body.

"What's going on?" I say, rub my eyes, and try to fully wake up.

"I've missed you … And your body." He slips on the bed with me and begins to kiss me on the lips, my neck, and my chest. His plump lips find one of my nipples and he licks it. He pulls my summertime shorts and underwear down and away from my body, drops them to the bedroom floor. I feel him between my legs, inside his mouth and throat, growing hard ... hard ... harder.

He's horny. He's always been a satisfying lover. Good in bed. A promising lover. Above average. I crave his face on my dick, and his fingers as they toy with my balls. He's a master at making love. Diligent. Extraordinary. He's rocked my world every time we have sex together. Not once has he been a slacker. Never.

# LABOR

I feel two of his fingers against my rump: rubbing here, toying with the tight slit, and turning me on. One of their tips enters me, stays inside. His mouth continues to work my dick over: juts his head up and down, licks and laps the tool, adding much suction. I moan beneath him, groan, mumble, and become lethargic, under his physical spells.

His unexpected labor becomes intense, desired, impulsive, and action that I have missed. After all, we *are* boyfriends … lovers. We have been for two years. I become drunk on his needs, and drunk on my own needs as our rawness continues on the bed. I'm not inebriated, knowing exactly what happens and unfolds between us, comprehending everything: touching, licking, and sucking between men who care deeply for each other.

And now, rather instantly, he pulls his face away from my center, but he continues to keep his one finger inside me, twisting it left and right, slipping it deeper inside, pulling it out, slipping it inside again, twisting it left and right again.

# *I NO HURT YOU*

And ... And ... And Finn enters my bedroom: fully naked, fully hard between his legs, fully smiling from ear to ear. Beautiful. The man is one of the most beautiful humans I have ever seen. Pale and chiseled. Blond and blue-eyed. Muscular from toes to head. X-shaped in the center. God-like. Someone I can stare at for the rest of my life and have my tongue hang out. I want to fuck him, or have him fuck me. Whatever.

He walks up to the bed and leans over my body. He kisses one of my nipples, the other one. He brushes a palm through my hair and says in broken English, perhaps hypnotizing me, "I no hurt you, Karl." It's something he always says to me. He adds more kisses to my nipples. Both of them. *Both!*

I don't push Finn away. I *allow* him to apply kisses to my chest, reach for my veined stick, and provide the mass of meat with a tug, two tugs, and three tugs. I *let* him give the post three quick sucks. And I want him to *stay ... stay ... stay*.

The men share my dick. One sucks. The other sucks. I feed them both what they want as they take turns on me, hungry for me. All of me.

Thank God Finn does stay. Finn Phluger doesn't go anywhere. Because we are meant to be a threesome. Together. I give him permission to stay because he's a hot motherfucker who swings his right leg over my naked torso, slaps his drooping balls against my left cheek, and pushes the tip of his firm cock inside my mouth. Before I know what happens, we're sucking each other, doing a sixty-nine position. And my boyfriend is busy at work, lubing my bottom with some K-Y, preparing me for some dick-to-ass action that I know he's a king at.

# SOUNDS

Oh my God! It's a top-notch threesome. A human puzzle on my bed. Guy-with-guy-with-guy. Interlocking men. I have Finn's dick in my mouth, his blond balls slap against my eyes and forehead, and my boyfriend slides his condom-covered dick inside me, fucking me. Finn blows me while this happens. I am totally being taken advantage of by both men, but don't seem to mind. Not in the slightest. In fact, the two men become a drug for me. We glide apart, together again, smack each other with our mouths and pricks, and fill my bedroom with the most pornographic sounds imaginable: woofs, grunts, slaps, a howl or two, and a long string of explicit names that one will never hear in church or at a mother's table.

# WEST HOLLYWOOD

I admit, time becomes lost. Seconds and minutes tick by and I feel like I'm in H. G. Wells' *The Time Machine*. I don't know if we fuck around for ten minutes … twenty-three minutes … or an hour. All I know is that I gag beneath Finn's weight, chocking on his cock as he bangs his big knob in my face-hole. I feel his mouth on my prized tool, sucking on it, manipulating the piece of beef, and willing me to blow my load, not in his mouth, but on his cheek or neck. I have Corbin's plunger inside me, banging … banging … banging at my opening, plugging me with his mass as he holds my ankles, and coaching *our* "new" boyfriend, "Suck him off, Finn. Suck him hard. I want him to wash your face down with cream."

I've seen all the adult movies I can see in my thirty-four years. And I've acted out a few. But nothing … nothing has ever happened to me like this threesome. I've always been a one-with-one-man-in-the-sack. A two-man under the sheets guy. Any man that knows me realizes I'm not into threesomes, foursomes, orgies, dick- or ass-parties, or the common pile-ups that occur among men in a group. I'm quiet boring when it comes to sexual relations with a man. Dull and uneventful. Let's just say that West Hollywood and the queer film crews/industry, and their XXX directors aren't hunting me down to be an actor. No way.

But … but I turn into a sex monster on the bed. A porn king or god. I take what's given to me and enjoy every minute of it. And I give it back to the two men just as they give it to me. It's like I've done threesomes all my life. All. My. Life.

And I'm in love with Corbin and Finn. Both of them.

Love.

Love.

# *BLOW*

It happens. Of course it does. Do you think or believe it doesn't happen. Are you this stupid? I mean, come on! What the fuck? There's a threesome happening on my bed. Tons of nakedness. A lot of grunts and groans. Much friction among men as dicks slip into holes. Panting. Huffs. Puffs. And a pedigree German saying again and again, "Kommen … Kommen … Kommen," when he stops sucking on my dick, deciding to jack me off.

Yes. We ejaculate. *Together!*

Firstly, my boyfriend jacks his load into the condom that separates our bodies. He actually has tears in his eyes as he comes, and he bites his lower lip.

Secondly, the German comes. He pulls his dick out of my mouth, and washes a load down the right side of my face: over my cheek and neck and part of the upper area of my chest.

Lastly, I spray three arcs of white man-syrup out of my flag, over Finn's right shoulder because he still lies over my chest, and it splatters against his back.

A gooey job well done.

Kudos to the three of us.

Applaud now.

*Now!*

# THEY LEAVE

Post-sex. I feel physically drained, dizzy, and confused. Both men kiss me after the heated sex-session. Finn leaves my bedroom first, vanishing into the living room. He probably fetches his pile of clothes. Corbin stands over me, says down to me, "I love you, Karl. And Finn loves you. We'll be back for breakfast. Or at least I think we will. Rest up. You look like we did you in."

"Love you and …"

He places fingers to my mouth, shakes his head. "Tomorrow. It's getting late. Sleep for now." And he goes.

———

# JULY 17

# LUCY VISITS

It's still hot outside. Steeping like a tea kettle. Bursting with fire from hell. Blistering against the skin. The hottest days of summer on record. *Ever!* Trust me, take shade or you'll die from the heat.

Lucy looks over her lemon-iced water with the widest eyes I have ever seen. She checks on me, and wants to spend a moment of chitchat time with me. Plus, she needs to borrow my deodorant. She's out and doesn't want to buy any; even if the closest store is two blocks away. I'm her local grocery store when she's out of something. Toothpaste. Toilet paper. A bar of Dove. Paper towels. We sit across from each other in my tiny-tiny kitchen. I don't lie to her and walk her through my evening again. *Every* detail. Even how the three of us men come together, all at the same time.

"Jesus Christ. I leave you alone for a few hours and look what happens to your life."

I raise my eyebrows, shrug. The bubbling excitement of the previous evening still electrifies the surface of my skin. "I know. Right?"

She reaches across the all-white, two-person table in the all-white kitchen, and leashes one of my hands within her own. She squeezes it like an arm wrestler and stares me down. "Corbin brought the German over to your apartment and the two men seduced you?"

"That's exactly what happened." My heart still races because of the event. I'm still semi-hard under the table, thinking about it.

She contentedly sighs. "I'm jealous. I've always been into threesomes." She bites the tip of one nail. "Did you do threesomes before?"

"Not with Corbin in this relationship. Not until three weeks ago. I must admit, Finn has made this boyfriendhood with

Corbin more exciting. I thought it was over-the-top-hot that the two of them showed up and ... stirred me awake."

"I'm jealous again."

I dramatically nod, and laugh. "The German will stick around now. Certainly after last night."

"I would say so."

"You fall in love so easily, Karl. You always have."

"It's one of my flaws."

"We all have flaws. Your heart is so delicate."

"Everyone's is. You just know mine well. You always have."

"I do." She nods. "And other intimacies of your life."

"Hear. Hear," I say, raise my lime-iced water to hers, and we drink.

# HEAT

I work: continue to build *Princess Castle on Lake Erie* for two hours and sort through about three hundred photographs. I put the photographs into three piles: small, medium, and large lighthouses. Decide to pick out six and email the pics to Kim Shredder, who will know what to do with them in puzzleland.

It's hot. Too damn hot. Even inside. Thank God for the flat's air condition because I would fry to death since the temperature outside is 107. Sweltering. An inferno. Sweat bubbles on my forehead and the backs of my arms as I work. I try not to think about it and work … work … work.

# AUDITION - TONIGHT!

The doorbell on my flat rings three times, distracting me. *Ring. Ring. Ring.* I go to the door, open it, and see Cub (he lives one floor down) standing in the hallway.

Okay. Okay. This isn't his real name. His name is Chester Knight. But I call him Cub, because this is what he looks like: brown curly hair, matching eyes, close-cut beard, and a small frame. Cub is superiorly well-built, no shirt, hair between his pecs, treasure trail of thin hair beneath his navel, huge mound of beef in his tight jeans, no belt. He's twenty-three. Not a day older. Cub all the way.

"Mr. Meader," he says, stands with his fingers pressed inside his pockets, and his thumbs are in the denim's loops. He raises his shoulders and looks about as adorable as ever in his bare feet. He grins from ear to ear, happy to see me.

"Cub, what's up?" I stand at the door and hold it open.

"Are we on for this evening?"

*On? This? Evening?* I wonder what he's talking about. *Think, Karl. Think. What is he talking about? What are you forgetting?*

He adorably tilts his head to the right, grins his magic; a young man's smile that probably beds his gentleman lovers with ease, and says, "Practice for my porn audition. This evening at eight. It's still on here in your flat, right?"

It hits me like a punch. I've obviously forgotten. "Yes. Yes. Yes. Eight o'clock. Of course it's still on. I didn't forget."

Cub wants to audition for adult films. The newly established company is called Manhandling Incorporated. His audition is a week away. He needs some practice acting in front of the camera and I have agreed to have him—let me share a light cough here—act out a jackoff scene in my flat. Corbin, who works at WTMP (a local television channel) as a stage hand, has film experience, and will run the camera, while Finn and I will be Cub's two-person audience. Cub will take matters into his own hands—another light cough here—and manipulate his seven-inch dick for fifteen minutes in front of the camera, attempting to ease his nerves as an adult film performer. Bottom line: he'll moan and groan, stroke beef a few times, smile a lot, get his jollies off, and eventually jack his load onto his chest. Fingers crossed.

"Eight it is then. I won't disappoint," he says.

"I'm sure you won't," I reply.

And off he goes, back to his flat, flaunting his tight, doable, and bulbous bottom.

# SURPRISE VISIT

Cub vanishes and another visitor arrives at the flat, interrupting my day: Finn. He pulls me away from my work, steps inside my flat, and closes the door behind him. He says something in German that I don't understand, grinning from ear to ear. In broken English, while kissing me on my cheek, he mumbles, "I like see you and visit you ... Kiss you ... Eat you."

Positioned near the closed door, I ... I feel his hands on my shorts, which he pulls down to my ankles. He falls to his knees. I immediately embrace the smooth warmth of his mouth over my already hardening tool and his head starts to slowly swing back and forth; an action I have gotten used to lately. He begins to suck me off and gently squeezes my balls. He slurps and sucks on my dick, adding impressive suction.

I think of the night before: Finn-Corbin-me. I think of how our bodies twisted-molded-tangled together as Finn's head bobs forward and backward. I think of his cock in my mouth and my cock in his mouth last night and how Corbin banged, banged, banged me, and …

"I can't help it … Coming," I say, feel overexcited, and pull out of his throat and mouth, and unload a creamy smear against his left cheek, down and along his throat, decorating his white-white skin.

He laughs, loving his treasure, exactly what he has come for, looking up at me, glowing. "What I wanted."

And he leaves, just as quickly as he arrives, with two paper towels in his hands, for cleanup. His mission accomplished: only to pleasure me. Winks at me, says, "Goodbye and thank you."

Gone. So quickly. Gone.

# LONG STORY

An hour later I text Corbin: *Got an amazing blowjob from the German. Squirted on his cheek. Damn hot. Does he really have to go back to Germany to visit his family? What if he doesn't come back? Can't he stay with us forever? We must keep him. I'm falling for him. I'm talking in love.*

I see Cub on Piffin Street again. Many floors down. So small. Like a speck. Hardly visible to the eye. In his jeans and a T-shirt. Has a murse over a shoulder. Six floors down. There. Attracting me. Mine for the taking if I want him. To share with Corbin and Finn. I have to hurry if I want him. A catch. A must.

Try to take the elevator down to the lobby. It stops on five. Some stud walks inside that looks like a young Brad Pitt. Looks delicious in a pair of running shoes and shorts. Nothing more. "You're huffing," he says. "Your face is red. Are you alright? Did you just have sex or something?"

"On a mission."

"What kind of mission?"

"Long story."

He winks at me, obviously flirting. "I have time for a long story."

"You're gorgeous … but another time."

The elevator falls to the lobby. Opens. I step out and rush through the glass-steel-onyx lobby. Bolt onto Puffin, into the blistering sunshine. Hot. Too hot. The sunshine can kill vampires; it's this hot.

# FOLLOW CUB

His pace slows and I see him make a right turn on West Blier Street. I follow him, as I have every intention to do so. I close the gap between us and become closer and closer to him. Forty feet becomes thirty feet. Thirty feet becomes twenty feet. And twenty feet becomes ten feet. This short distance causes me to study his frame more: mighty muscles here and there, meaty thighs and arms, and shoulders of steel. The man's ass is tight: two impressively rounded orbs, tightly compact, smackable, a delicious looking rump. The murse at his right side looks stuffed, also bulging like his rump. His sneakers thump-thump against the sidewalk as he walks.

I watch him turn to the right, up a set of four steps, into the Pearson & Lodge building through a revolving door. He passes the security desk to his right and yells out to the female guard on duty, "Good afternoon, Penny!"

Penny nods, playing on her phone. She barely waves at him.

From afar, as he heads to the elevator bay in the distance, I make out his boyish face. So cute. Charming. One of the six elevators opens and he steps inside. Vanishes.

Before leaving, I go to the office building's directory near the four, stand-alone front doors, and the large revolving door which we came through. I see Cub's father's name on the directory: *Dr. Kade Knight, Child Psychiatrist.*

Impressive.

Very impressive.

# PREPARATIONS

Evening. The day is still volcanic hot.
Steeping hot. Planet Mercury hot. It doesn't
stop me from prepping for Cub's practice
audition and guests. I clean the flat from top
to bottom, run down to the deli and pick up
some picnic things to eat (three different
types of breads, two seafood salads, meats
and cheeses, two dips, cold crab legs), and
create a foodies spread that I think everyone
will enjoy. I also end up at the spirits store
and pick up a few bottles of wine,
champagne, and a fresh bottle of
Jagermeister for Finn, which is his favorite.

Hereafter, I arrange proper seating in
front of the sofa to watch the audition: two
reading chairs and one stiff and high-back
chair from the kitchen table setting. I form a
half circle and provide enough room for

Corbin to operate his Canon XA11 camera with high definition and a composite output.

I also place a stack of freshly washed and dried towels next to the sofa for Cub's use and a quick cleanup. There are five towels in all. Cream-colored to match the juice that is expected to churn out of his meaty spike.

A perfect plan.

Now to execute the evening.

Here goes.

Ready. Set. Go.

Hang on for the ride.

It may be bumpy … and sticky.

# THE STRAY

Guests arrive around seven, an hour before Cub's show. Corbin and Finn first. Now Cub from downstairs. Of course, Lucy is invited, but she is on a date with Lee. The pair is at a séance, somewhere in Ohio at her Uncle Pete's. I'm sure I'll hear the details about this adventure later.

A fourth, *unexpected,* guest arrives. Cub's boyfriend. His name is Cyrus Weston. Some adorable and lanky country bumpkin from West Virginia with ginger hair, green eyes, a pierced nose, and the sexiest twang in his voice that can probably drop any man to his knees.

Cyrus, probably twenty-two or -three, is a gentleman, raised properly by his single momma, apologies for intruding on the evening without an invitation, and adds, "I need to be here to support my boyfriend. Cub is nervous." I'm surprised he uses the name for my neighbor downstairs. Apparently it sticks. All nicknames should in my opinion, especially when I come up with them.

"It's fine," I tell him. "Perfectly fine. No worries." I decide to make Cyrus feel at home, give him a man-hug, squeeze him against me, tight and compact, and pass him off to Corbin and Finn, for two more man-hugs, comforting him, welcoming the stray to an evening of fun and cum.

# FOODIES FIRST

It's unanimous: we decide to have a foodies feast first and Cub's practice audition second. The spread is like a smorgasbord and the men go hog wild, acting like animals. They go *oink, oink, oink* all over their shit. Not that I mind since this is why I buy the provisions, hoping they eat like men, enjoying themselves. I mean, isn't this why we're all here?: Cub, Cyrus, Corbin, Finn, and me. All of us. Woofing this food down as if it is our last meal. Hungry as wolves.

# APPROVAL

I do have a private one-on-one with Cyrus before his boyfriend's man-show starts. We stand near the impeccable view of the evening's blue-green Lake Erie water as we hold drinks. He chooses a beer and I prefer a white wine. We clink the beverages together in a toast and he says, "To my lover's success this evening."

"But of course," I reply.

Following a sip of his beer, he admits, "My man is going to knock this out of the park. He's a pro at jacking off, but what guy isn't?"

It's a doorway for me to ask the most important question of all regarding his relationship with Cub, "Do you support your boyfriend being in adult films?"

Wide-green eyes stare at me with a broad, fall-into smile. "I support anything Cub does."

"You do know he's going to be kissing other guys," I clear my throat and continue with, "among other *things*, right?"

He nods, looking innocent and naïve.

"May I be frank, Cyrus?"

"Yes. Of course."

"You're going to be fine watching your boyfriend suck another man's dick, ride various hard cocks, and do unthinkable things with sex toys and XXX male performers?"

Cyrus continues to grin at me, leans close to my right ear, places one of his palms flat against my stomach, and confesses, "It's a total turn on for me to watch my man with another man, or other men. I crave nothing less."

Enough said. He leaves me open-mouthed, stunned. It's a big *wow!* for me. But I accept it just the same. To each his own.

# THE SHOW BEGINS

The show begins shortly after we make pigs of ourselves regarding the food and fresh drinks. Cub doesn't seem nervous at all, but I bet he is. He enters the living room wearing a white T-shirt and jeans, but no socks. He looks good in the easy-to-remove outfit as he sits down in the middle of the sofa.

To my left, Corbin works the camera. To my right, Finn stares at the sofa and Cub as if he is about to watch an Academy Award-winning movie. Standing behind me is Cub's boyfriend, Cyrus, who smells like hummus and wienies wrapped in freshly baked dough.

The room goes quiet and still. Corbin instructs Cub, "Do your thing, man. Act like none of us is here. Have at yourself. Action!"

# *NOT AN AMATUER*

I admit here and now: Cub isn't an amateur at acting and ... jerking off. He's been in front of the camera before and works it like a pro. He seductively peels his T-shirt off, loses it on the floor next to his feet, licks his fingertips with his extended tongue, presses the tips to his nipples, and makes the pair grow hard. As if he has accomplished this task a thousand times, he rolls his right palm down the ripped and narrow structure of his bumpy and pumped chest, makes a circular motion around his navel with the palm, and begins to unbutton his jeans, one button at a time while jutting his hips upwards.

# FLEXES HIS MUSCLES

Of course Cub toys with the camera, and his viewers. He massages his tube of underwear-covered tool after removing his denim: up and down with his right palm, his left palm, both palms, smiling from ear to ear in Corbin's direction. He flexes his muscles like a model (thighs, biceps, abs), winks at the camera, and moves slowly while accomplishing his master work. Erotically he rubs his center until his dick is completely firm, removes his cotton briefs, and drops them to the floor with his jeans and T-shirt. How simply he becomes naked on the sofa and continues his solo show, proving that he might just land a role as an adult performer.

# HOLE

I'm impressed that Cub can swing his knees up to his shoulders and show off his smooth and hairless hole to us. The taut hole winks at us: once, twice, three times. It causes my center to become damp with a pre-bubble of jiz, which leaks out of my dick's head; obvious excitement because of the scene.

I also become excited that he uses two fingertips on the hole, pushing the pair inside himself. He moans and groans, and tells the camera, "I can't wait to come. Do you want to watch me come?" Winks.

As he fingers himself with one hand, he uses his other hand on his shaft. The tool is a swollen, veined, and an upright mass that literally pulses, ready to burst between his pumped thighs. He manhandles both areas as he growls, pumps his hips upwards, falls, pumps upwards again, and continues to pleasure himself for the next few minutes.

# TENTS

Tents form around me. Corbin is hard behind his camera. To my right, Finn hides his erection with his left hand, but it's hopeless because everyone can see its pumped hugeness. The country boy, Cyrus, is still positioned behind me. He has his wood out and plays and pumps the fleshy beast. His left hand juts up and down and his cheeks puff. He's captivated by the scene on the sofa, bulging, panting, and his eyes are wide open. I've never seen a dude into his boyfriend so much. Maybe he's in love. It's like Corbin, Finn and I aren't even in the room.

# *OOZE*

Cub, half seated and half lying on the sofa, continues to thrust his hips upwards, they fall, upwards again, they fall, upwards. Perspiration in beads bedazzle the area of hair on his chest, and his thighs. The young man's nipples look like torpedoes. Moans and groans escape his lungs. His right hand rockets up and down on his meat. He mumbles something I can't understand, huffs, and …

Spirals of thick and white goo fly out of his cock's head and splatter against his chest, decorating his thin weave of brown fur. Some of the goop clings to his right hand and the helmet of his dick. Within seconds, he begins to feed himself all of the ooze, licking the cream off his drizzled fingertips, one by one. He looks directly into the camera, seductively smiles at his viewers, still bone-hard between his legs, giggles, and ends his scene. Fin.

# IT'S NOT OVER

"It's not over," Cyrus says. "Keep the camera running, but keep my face out of the shot." He steps out from behind me, peels out of his clothes, drops material to the living room floor, and steps up to his boyfriend on the sofa.

I look at Corbin and he looks at me. We both shrug at the same time. I mouth to him, "Film it," and Corbin nods.

My attention steers to Cyrus' body. He's beautiful for being extra-thin. Quite skeletal, but extraordinarily stunning. What I'm impressed most about the country boy is his dick's length: a long nine inches. No shit. The thing is *huge*.

Even Finn notices his cock's size. Finn's mouth hangs open at the sight of it, completely surprised.

# "SUCK IT."

Positioned next to the sofa, Cyrus plants himself sideways so Corbin gets a shot of his long shaft and dangling balls. He stands in front of Cub's face. "Suck it," he demands of Cub, pivoting the audition to a new and different level. "And don't be shy, man. Take it all down your throat."

Cub isn't shy by any means. Not in the slightest. I can tell that this isn't the first time he has eaten all nine inches of Cyrus' country boy cock. No way. Cub literally takes the flag down the back of his throat with ease. No problem at all. He doesn't gag or choke. He doesn't squirm or lose oxygen. It's as if he is meant to take the long guy-spike inside his mouth and throat, and carefully breathes through his nose.

# STAR

Of course, Cyrus holds the back of his boyfriend's head and thwaps Cub's face with his meat.

*Thwap. Thwap. Thwap.*

Of course, his drooping balls slap against Cub's chin and part of his neck as Cyrus vibrantly and chaotically bangs the wannabe porn star's boyish looks.

*Thwap. Thwap. Thwap.*

Of course, Cyrus keeps quiet above Cub, except for a few grunts and huffs, because the camera is still rolling.

*Thwap. Thwap. Thwap.*

Of course, Cub acts like a professional, seated on the edge of the sofa, mouth lodged with a huge dick, one hand now toying with Cyrus' balls, his other hand rolling up and along his man's thin chest, ready to pinch a nipple.

# A GENTLE TUG

The porn star pair continues this mouth-to-cock action for the next few minutes. Not that Finn gets bored with the deed since I see him rub the material-covered dick between his legs a number of times.

At one point, Finn catches me looking at him and he reaches for my right hand. He gently tugs it to his center, rolls it over his dick, and mouths to me, being silent, "Jack me off, man."

"Unzip it," I mouth to him, nodding.

He goes for it and I slip my hand around his bloated tool, wanting to get him off and feel his spew on my fingers and palm.

# MASSIVE JOINT

My gaze moves from the two boyfriends on the sofa to my action on Finn's dick. It's as if I'm watching a basketball game take place. Back and forth. Back and forth. Back and forth. In the process, my right hand continuously juts up and down, causing friction with Finn's massive joint. My fingers feel the inflated veins along his cum-filled spike. Excess skin rolls along my appendages, up and down. Light sounding puffs escape the German next to me as he gently and smoothly humps my hand, rising off his seat, also watching the twosome on the sofa, and me.

# PROFESSIONAL BY ALL MEANS

Because of Cub's work in front of the camera, I'm honestly not surprised that Finn shoots his load quickly. Truth is, Cub goes to town on Cyrus-knob at the front of the room. It's enough for any man—even a straight one—to churn up a load and blow it everywhere within seconds. Cub is a maximum cocksucker extraordinaire. It's a wonder he doesn't lose consciousness and fall to the floor while blowing Cyrus, needing emergency care because of his boyfriend's big trophy dick. But the man's a professional by all means, and takes it just like he wants it: all of it down his throat, and Cyrus' balls *thwapping* against his chin again and again and again.

# SHOOT-MESS

As expected, after Finn releases a soft whimper, juts his hips upwards another time, white sap arcs out of the German's spike and decorates his shirt and shorts and my hand. It's a vat of man-butta' and goes everywhere. Never have I seen so much goop in one sitting. I'm not sure if it's because of my up and down hand motion on his hammer, or Cub's mouthy work on Cyrus' shaft. Hell, it might just be both. Who knows? All I really know is that a shoot-mess occurs between Finn's legs and on my hand.

Spent and obviously pleased, glowing with a smile from my handy labor, Finn quietly leaves my side and heads to the bathroom for a cleanup. As for the gooey mess on my right appendage, I take matters into my own hands, decide a German man-snack will do me some good, and feast on Finn's creamy bittersweet load that I wear on my fingers and right wrist, relishing his masculine flavor.

*Yum!*

# GYMNAST

Back to the show at hand: Cub's porn audition. The boyfriends on the sofa change positions. Cub used to be a gymnast in high school and … I can tell. Corbin can also probably tell. And when Finn returns to the living room … he'll too be able to tell.

Here's why Cub's a gymnast this evening: he leans over the side of the sofa with one foot propped up on its arm and the other foot planted on the floor. His ass is pointed out and upwards, ready for Cyrus' use. In fact, while the camera still rolls, Cyrus rubs the tip of his long and hard dick against his boyfriend's pink-tight asshole, teasing the young man.

Cub loves the action and calls out, "More. Let me have it."

Cyrus slaps his slab of nine inches against Cub's slit: once, twice, three times.

And Cub begs, "Fuck me, man. Fuck me already. I want you inside me."

# A DEMAND

This "Fuck me, man," and cock-slapping game continues for a minute until the German returns to his seat beside me. He is all cleaned up, grinning from ear to ear, happy to be a part of the audience again.

Over the sofa, Cub is spanked by Cyrus, both with the slender man's dick and his right hand.

Corbin continues to film, a constant tent formed between his legs.

Acting, or maybe not, Cub demands over his left shoulder, "Put your dick inside me. All nine inches of it. Do it now."

Cyrus responds by slapping his pick against Cub's needy hole: once, twice, three times. He doesn't say anything in return. Not that he has to.

# INCH BY INCH

I determine quite clearly that this has definitely happened numerous times in their relationship, prior to this moment:

One inch of Cyrus' dick enters Cub's bottom and Cub squints.

Two inches cause him to grunt.

Three inches make him jostle forward a touch over the sofa.

Four inches spear his rear and he growls.

"Yes … More," Cub groans as five inches plummet inside him.

Six inches lock his hub and he grits his teeth.

Seven inches slide mercilessly inside his rump and he hangs on the side of the sofa for dear life, I only assume that he hopes not to fall to the floor.

A look of terror unfolds on Cub's face as eight hard inches pump his gap.

Nine whole inches of lance pierces his end, stops at its hilt, and prompts tears to line the corners of Cub's eyes.

# BANGING

"Fuck yes … Yes … Yes," Cub acts in front of the camera, being pounded by the country boy behind him. "Give me all of it. Don't be nice to me. Bang me. And bang me hard."

It's not an act. It can't be. I won't believe that it is. These two bang like this all the time. It's probably why they are together. A couple made in heaven.

*Banging.*

*Banging.*

*Banging.*

Cub gets nailed like the porn star he wants to be. All nine inches of Cyrus slide into him, pull out, and slide inside him again

… again … and again. Their banging and connection is relentless. They are unstoppable as their bodies hit together, separate, and hit together again, repeatedly.

# CONSIDERABLE
# PAIN

Cub grunts, groans, growls, and mumbles. He hangs on to the sofa as if his life is in danger. His asshole is split open as his lover's—they have to be *lovers!*, I think— nine inches continue to play havoc with it. Cub cringes and cries. Cub digs his fingers into the sofa's material as he is being fucked … fucked … fucked, and Cyrus' balls *thwap* against his thighs. Honestly, Cub looks as if he is in considerable pain in front of the country boy, yet loving every second of the man-feast at the same time.

And this action continues for the next ten … thirteen … eighteen minutes as they come together, fall apart, and come together again and again and again.

# LIKE A HORSE

Eventually Cyrus pulls his condom-covered dick out of his buddy, boyfriend, lover and whispers to Cub, "Sit on my dick now. Ride me like a horse." He positions himself on the center of the sofa and pats his lap. The upright flag between his legs swings to left and to the right just like the flag pole it is. He holds it still, and nods at Cub to continue his act. "You know what to do."

Corbin looks at me. I look at him. The both of us smile at each other. To my right, Finn grabs my right thigh, provides it a firm squeeze, perhaps also on the edge of his seat, continuing to enjoy the evening's show/audition.

# DROP ON IT

Again, this audition is about Cub and Cub only. This is why he faces the camera, blocking the view of Cyrus' chest and face. The only physical attributes we can see of the country boy are his thighs, dangling balls, and condom-covered nine-inch dick.

Cub grins at us, his audience. There's a hungry look on his face as he positions his hole over Cyrus' lever and begins to drop on it. Inch by inch by inch. In doing so, he grits his teeth and squeezes his eyes closed. Frankly, he takes it like the man he is, though. Before we realize it, he has all nine inches of the stick inside his torso and he's sitting against Cyrus, bottom against pelvic bone, ready to begin something rather special, beautiful, and photogenic between them.

# RISES. FALLS.

Manhandling Incorporated will be quite pleased to see Cub in his audition film because he performs most of the work, just as the porn actor he wants to be. He literally rises and falls on his boyfriend's rod again and again.

Rises. Falls. Rises. Falls.

Their balls sometimes slap together because of the motion. And the splatter of fur on Cub's chest grows sweaty by all standards of the word.

Rises. Falls. Rises. Falls.

Cub growls and arches his back. He moans and rolls a hand up and down his chest. He pinches both nipples with both hands. He …

Rises. Falls. Rises. Falls.

Rises. Falls. Rises. Falls.

Rises. Falls. Rises. Falls.

# KUDOS

Pleasure and pain is seen on Cub's face as he rides Cyrus' cock. Perhaps I'm surprised by this, but honestly, I'm not. The men are boyfriends, of course. *Lovers.* This isn't their first sexual adventure. Cub has probably ridden Cyrus' nine inches numerous times before.

But … it still doesn't mean Cub isn't in pleasure and pain. Pleasure because his ass is enjoying the country boy's dick, and also pain because I see that his eyes are locked closed, as well as his teeth. Both actions tell me that he's maybe being less gentle with Cyrus' tool than he usually is when the two men fuck around.

*Whatever.* The audition is top-notch shit. Whoever is going to watch will love it.

The faceless country boy is being an excellent supporting actor, and Cub is killing it as the star. Kudos to both men and their dicks.

Fucking kudos all the way!

# A SECOND COMING

If grappling his rod and jacking its meat up and down in his right fist, while rising and falling on Cyrus' cock, doesn't get Cub the porn star job, I don't know what will.

I know … I know Cub has every intention of coming a second time during this homemade flick. I would surely do the same thing if I were in his position. Hell yes I would!

Cub rises and falls, rises and falls, and jacks himself off with a speedy palm and fingers. Somewhat semi-unconscious he arches his back and satisfies his bottom and his dick at the time. Sweat flies off the young man here and there. Grunts fill the room as he tugs on his extension of meat. And chaos builds and builds as he announces to his viewers (*us*) and the camera, "I can't help myself. I'm going to come again."

# JACKS

Cub stops rising and falling. He stays still on his partner's shaft. This show isn't over, though. No way. Not by a long shot. Cub jacks … jacks … jacks his tool up and down … shows off his bursting muscular tone, makes an animal-like grunt, and releases his second load on his chest in an unforgettable performance. A five-star extravaganza. Splatter. Splatter. Splat.

Three strings of the white shit glaze his nipples and bear-like pecs. The gunk hangs in his hair like snow on a pine tree. One thinks its quantity is less than his first blow, but it doesn't look this way. No sir. The white jiz is everywhere on the man's pecs. A vat of the stuff. A white wonderland of sorts. Wet velvet. Liquid snow.

# ON YOUR BACK

Cyrus is not going to end the scene without ejaculating his load. Hell no. He smacks Cub's bottom and whispers, "Get on your back, man."

Cub rises off Cyrus' spike, limp between his legs, probably dizzy and somewhat semi-conscious, and helps his boyfriend up and off the sofa. He listens to Cyrus and lays down on his back, face-up, still sticky and cum-covered. His head is near one of the sofa's arms.

Cyrus whispers, "Lay the other way, with your head near the center of the sofa. I'll kneel on the cushions. I want your face between my legs. I have a treat for you."

The wide grin that covers Cub's face is adorable. It will surely cause viewers to fall in love with him and land him a contract in the porn industry. Truth is, he'll do well in making adult films, being a top or bottom, whatever they want from him, doing his best in front of the camera, and using the tools that he has to offer.

# HUNGRY FOR IT

Cyrus kneels on the sofa, swings his right leg over Cub's head, and slaps his dangling balls against his boyfriend's forehead. He shares a laugh, finds the moment funny, and perhaps excitable.

Cub looks as if he doesn't mind that Cyrus' balls thwap against the top of his head and in his eyes. Nor does he look as if he minds that Cyrus is jacking his nine-inch meat over his opened mouth, readying to blow his load inside. It's expected now since Cyrus kneels behind him on the sofa, with Cub's head between the supporting actor's legs.

Cub anticipates Cyrus bursting his load and says, "Shoot it in my mouth. I'm hungry for it. Give it to me."

Cyrus bolts his hips to and fro, busy with his right hand, and works his tool. He huffs, steady with his breathing. He puffs. He grunts. He fucks his hand and becomes persistent, *thwapping* ... *thwapping* ... *thwapping* his balls against Cub's head and in his eyes.

# CREAM

"Come now. Come inside me," Cub begs, and licks his lips. "I want to eat what you have to give me."

As if on cue, no longer capable of holding his load inside, Cyrus bolts his hips forward one last time and ...

Cream floods over Cub's face. It covers his nose, his forehead, drips over his closed eyes, and sprays inside his semi-opened mouth. Cyrus blows load after load of his white and oppressive cargo on his boyfriend's features, washing him down, covering his face in the thick, paint-like substance and he huffs ... huffs ... huffs, emptying his balls through his dick. Spent.

# SUCKING SPENT

Cub drags Cyrus' cream inside his mouth with two fingertips. He laps at the goo, eating it all up, removing it from his skin. The amateur porn star gobbles up the goop as if it is the bitter and sweetest treat on the planet, devouring the substance until it's completely gone, bare from his face.

He also licks the country boy's stiff club clean, sucking spent from it. One suck. Two sucks. Three sucks. Until there isn't a single drop of the spew left on the pick. Cub eats all of the ejaculate up, hungry for the man-sap. Desirous for Cyrus' seed. All of it. All. Of. It. Until it is gone. Vanished.

# *THANKS*

The scene ends with Cub laughing on the sofa and Corbin turning off the camera. His laughter stops and he smiles from ear to ear. He continues to smile until Corbin yells, "Cut! … That's a wrap!"

Cub yawns and stretches. He's exhausted on the sofa now that the scene/audition is over. He calls out, "Corbin, thanks for filming us. And Karl, thanks for letting us use your living room. And Finn … I saw that you got jacked by Karl. Way to go, man. Good job. Nicely executed."

Finn shares the longest and proudest smile.

"I saw that too," Corbin admits. "I almost stopped filming and joined you two. I wanted jacked off."

"And thanks, babe!" Cub calls out to his country boy. "You were the bomb. Your dick was magic during the scene. If I get a job with Manhandling, it's going to be because of you."

# PLAN

Cub and Cyrus kiss as lovers often do. Their sticky bodies entwine. Their tongues connect. They give off a warm ambiance inside the living during the kiss.

Following the kiss, the pair oppose to my suggested quick cleanup process with the cotton towels that I have set aside for them. Instead, Cub says, "Anyway we can just jump in your shower? We'll do a quick soap-down and rinse, climb in our clothes, and party with you guys for the next few hours."

"Sounds like a plan," I tell them.

And so this is done.

# SHOWERS

Corbin has the camera running again. He stands outside my bathroom and films the almost-porn star and his boyfriend in the shower. The pair inside the shower soap each other's hard cocks with a bar a Dove.

I tap him on the shoulder and say, "You should maybe give them their own space and privacy. What do you say?"

"Maybe they want to be secretly filmed. I can give it to them for Christmas."

It's not a bad idea, but I tell him, "Forget about it. Let them be. Come with me and have a drink."

Corbin agrees, pulls his attention away from the shower scene, shuts off the camera, and follows me into the kitchen for a fresh drink, and the company of our sexy sidekick/boyfriend/lover—the German.

# THE PARTY
# CONTINUES

Cub and Cyrus exit the shower smelling of fresh soap, suds, and shampoo. They slip into their clothes again and the party continues. We gather in the kitchen, around the table, and share drinks and conversation. Everyone discusses Cub's evening audition.

Finn calls it, "Reines kunstwerk," which means *pure artwork* in German.

Corbin calls it, "A masterpiece in the making. It will definitely land you the job, Cub."

And I call it, "Sexy work alone, and with each other. Both of you did amazing things in front of the camera."

We all toast. Smiles are shared. Drinks are emptied. And more drinks are poured. The fun continues.

# SLOPPY DRUNKS

Events get crazy at the post-audition party. Shots are fired into mouths. Beer bottles clink together. Finn teaches a German drinking game. It turns into bedlam all around, and we have the time of our lives, celebrating the audition, couplehood, trupplehood, and endearing friendship.

I'm not surprised when the star of the evening, Cub, overdoes it with his booze content and rushes off to the bathroom. He kneels over the toilet and yacks into the bowl. Cyrus isn't much help, but he's behind him, being a supporter, saying again and again, in slurred English, "Yoush gosh ish," which I interpret as *you got this*.

As for Finn, Corbin, and me, we all party it up, and hard, but not like Cub. Cub plays on a level of his own by almost blacking out.

# *LEAVING TIME*

Every good party ends at its highest moment of fun. This is when Corbin becomes frisky with Finn in the bedroom. Cyrus and I stand in the living room and hear the two grunt and moan like beasts in the wild.

"What's going on in there?" Cyrus asks, less inebriated than I believe.

I joke, "I'm sure they're moving furniture. Finn always likes to redecorate."

"They're not moving furniture," Cyrus admits, shaking his head.

Of course not. I can only imagine what my two lovers are doing in the buff with their well-built and trim bodies. I shrug, and answer, "You never know."

"Well, whatever it is, Cub and I should let you join the pair. You need to have at your men. We should leave."

Golden words to my ears. I've never heard anything better. Scoot now. Be gone. The sounds from the bedroom grow more intense, wild, and louder. Plus, they're causing a boner between my legs.

"It was nice having you two. The whole evening was a blast, Cyrus. Can you and Cub make it downstairs safely?" A host always asks about the wellbeing of their guests, even if it's only one floor down.

"Sure. Sure. Sure. We'll be fine. Thank you again."

"My pleasure. Of course. So much fun," I tell him.

And they begin their exit as Cyrus picks his boyfriend up and off the sofa by his arms, tells him they are leaving. Off the pair go, into the night, out of the flat, to leave me alone with my masculine animals, growing wood, and spirited needs.

# CLEANUP

Cleanup can and will happen in the morning. I'm too exhausted to worry about the plates, glasses, bottles of wine, and other whatnots after the party ends. Although the place looks as if a tornado has passed through, it can wait. It's been a long evening of fun and cum, but now it's time for bed and sleep and …

Wrong. It's not time for bed and sleep. At least not yet. Corbin and Finn decide to spend the night at my flat because they have too much to drink. They are in the bedroom. Apparently they have other things on their minds before turning in for the night. The two are laughing. And I hear Corbin demand from our German lover, "Suck it, man. Put it in your mouth."

Finn replies in German. Something I don't understand. Never will.

And Corbin adds, "Damn, I really enjoy being inside your mouth."

# MUSCULAR SILHOUETTES

The thoughts of the two men getting it on with me make me hard. Maybe I'll watch them have at each other in the shadowy darkness: their muscular silhouettes slipping together and falling apart. Or I'll join in, creating a beautiful threesome. Who knows what the secrets of intimacy have in store for me, and them? For now, I lock the flat's front door and turn off all the lights. I head to the bedroom and my heated and passionate lovers. A very firm rise happens between my legs. Just as I suspect it will. A cordial and warm smile blooms on my face. Never have I been in love with such good men. Two men at once. Our blended trio. Us.

———

# EPILOGUE

# SPENT

My tale ends here, just as one expects. As if we have made love during these few pages, conclusions occur as well as middles and beginnings; the criteria of life. Listen…

A few very important post-intimate details need to be shared to resolve this unfinished business. Just to clear up some cum-stained areas from all this fun, shall I say?

Cub nails his live audition and lands a three-movie contract with Manhandling Incorporated. The movies are titled: *Pile-up! Business Men II. Be Afraid of Daddy.*

Cyrus is so proud of him. The two continue to be boyfriends and lovers. Cyrus does not decide to follow in Cub's footsteps and work for Manhandling, although he does love to watch his man having sex with other men, and confesses to me, "It's an aphrodisiac for me when I see Cub getting it on with other guys. Total kink stuff. I don't know why, but I absolutely love it. Most guys would be severely jealous. But not me. Strange, but true."

We celebrate Cub's win with another party. It's obnoxious. Over-the-top and out-of-this-world fun. We even invite some of his coworkers/friends from Manhandling and things become super wild, an orgy pile up, drugs, alcohol; another story for another time. Hang in there, you might just hear about it. *Wink. Wink.*

As for Finn … he returns to Germany for a month to visit his family, but comes back to the United States. Corbin and I keep him as a boyfriend. We find a bigger flat where all three of us can live together: happy, content, in love. It's what we want. Love is love. It happens sometimes among three handsome men. No doubt.

Lucy and Lee marry. Finn and I attend their wedding and reception. It's fabulous, just as I expect it to be. Corbin has to pull a shift at WTMP and can't get out of it. Poor bastard. Anyway, Lucy and Lee live a happy ever after story. She's pregnant now. Triplets. Good for them!

My final note here: having two men in life is better than one. Don't let anyone tell you different. Believe me, I know. Our trupple works out just fine for us. It's who we are, and who we've become. Man loves man loves man. I suggest trying it out for size. You might like it. You might not. But in the end, life is short and sweet and fun, and it's best not to look back on its unfolded pages and days, and ask, "Why didn't I do that?" So don't, my friend. Just don't. Play and have fun. Lots of fun.

———

# ABOUT THE AUTHOR

R. W. Clinger is a full-time writer in the Pittsburgh area. His hobbies include football, swimming and photography. R. W. is currently at work on a new novel.

# Also by R. W. Clinger

—

The Trainer
All the Pretty Boys
The Pool Boy
Timber
Firefly
Project 72
The Curious Neighbor
Tool
Tell Me Who You Are

Reach out to
R. W. Clinger at:

———

Facebook
Instagram
Twitter

146

Made in the USA
Monee, IL
01 August 2021

74718746R00085